6/13

Dear Parent:

Congratulations! Your child is taking the first steps on an exciting journey. The destination? Independent reading!

STEP INTO READING® will help your child get there. The program offers five steps to reading success. Each step includes fun stories and colorful art. There are also Step into Reading Sticker Books, Step into Reading Math Readers, Step into Reading Phonics Readers, Step into Reading Write-In Readers, and Step into Reading Phonics Boxed Sets—a complete literacy program with something for every child.

Learning to Read, Step by Step!

Ready to Read   Preschool–Kindergarten
• big type and easy words • rhyme and rhythm • picture clues
For children who know the alphabet and are eager to begin reading.

Reading with Help   Preschool–Grade 1
• basic vocabulary • short sentences • simple stories
For children who recognize familiar words and sound out new words with help.

Reading on Your Own   Grades 1–3
• engaging characters • easy-to-follow plots • popular topics
For children who are ready to read on their own.

Reading Paragraphs   Grades 2–3
• challenging vocabulary • short paragraphs • exciting stories
For newly independent readers who read simple sentences with confidence.

Ready for Chapters   Grades 2–4
• chapters • longer paragraphs • full-color art
For children who want to take the plunge into chapter books but still like colorful pictures.

STEP INTO READING® is designed to give every child a successful reading experience. The grade levels are only guides. Children can progress through the steps at their own speed, developing confidence in their reading, no matter what their grade.

Remember, a lifetime love of reading starts with a single step!

*To my Erik, who can fix
anything—even a bad day
—S.A.*

Step into Reading, Random House, and the Random House colophon are registered trademarks of Random House, Inc.

Visit us on the Web!
StepIntoReading.com
randomhouse.com/kids

Educators and librarians, for a variety of teaching tools, visit us at
RHTeachersLibrarians.com

ISBN: 978-0-7364-2889-7 (trade) — ISBN: 978-0-7364-8116-8 (lib. bdg.)

Printed in the United States of America   10 9 8 7 6

Disney

WRECK-IT RALPH

Game On!

By Susan Amerikaner

Illustrated by the Disney Storybook Artists

Random House 🏠 New York

Ralph and Felix live
in a video game.
Ralph wrecks things.
Wrecking is his job.

Felix fixes things

with his magic hammer.

Felix always wins a medal. Ralph never gets a medal.

Bad Guys do not

get medals.

Ralph wants

to be a Good Guy.

One day,
Ralph jumps
into a new game.

He gets a medal!

Ralph goes

to <u>Sugar Rush</u> next.

It is a racing game
in a candy world.

A little girl
takes Ralph's medal!
Her name is
Vanellope.
She is in a tree.

Ralph climbs the tree.

He wants

his medal back.

Vanellope wants to be
in the <u>Sugar Rush</u> race.
She needs a gold coin
to enter.
She uses Ralph's medal.

The winner will get
all the gold coins—
and Ralph's medal!

The other racers
do not want Vanellope
to race.

They wreck
her race kart.
They throw her
in the mud.

Ralph chases them away.
He will help Vanellope
win the race.
Then she will give
Ralph his medal back!

Ralph and Vanellope
make a new race kart.

King Candy tricks Ralph.
"Vanellope will get hurt
in the race,"
he says.

Ralph cannot
let Vanellope race!
The king gives Ralph
the gold medal.

Vanellope gives Ralph
a new medal.
She made it for him.

Ralph wants
to save Vanellope.

He wrecks her kart.

She cannot race.

She cannot get hurt.

Vanellope is sad.
King Candy
locks her
in a cell.

Ralph wrecks the wall.

He frees Vanellope.

Felix comes
to <u>Sugar Rush</u>.
Ralph and Felix
fix Vanellope's kart.

She wins the race!

Vanellope turns
into a princess!
She is the real ruler
of <u>Sugar Rush</u>.

Vanellope just wants
to be herself.
She thanks Ralph
for his help.

Ralph goes back
to his game.
He does not need a medal
to be a Good Guy.